To the beautiful and friendly people of Haiti.

ISBN 0-590-43494-2

12 11 10 9 8 7 6 5 4 3 2   9/8 0 1 2 3 4/9

Printed in the U.S.A.   08

Josephine's 'magination

A TALE OF HAITI

story and pictures by ARNOLD DOBRIN

SCHOLASTIC INC.
New York Toronto London Auckland Sydney

"If you're going to come with me to market you better get a move on," Josephine's mother called. Then she added—just in case Josephine might still dawdle on the way, "You hear me, girl? I'm going to market *now*."

Josephine put down her flower dolls and brushed the dirt off her skirt. She rushed into the house to get a drink of water, tried to brush some more dirt off her dress and then ran down the path. Already her mother was turning the bend in the road past the palmettos. Her back was straight as a board because on her head she carried the big basket of brooms she took each Friday morning to market.

Oh, it was hot—it was terribly hot! And it would be that way for a long time. It would stay that way through most of the day. But then, when the shadows started to get big, a cool, soft breeze would gently drift in from the sea. And that would feel so good.

About that time—if all the brooms were sold—Josephine's mother would give her some pennies to spend on whatever she wanted. Candy? Sweet jellied-rolls? It was always hard for Josephine to decide. But awfully nice to think about on and off throughout the day.

"Bonjour Lucille," said a woman who suddenly came out of a path on her way to town. She carried a heavy load of fruit to sell and already she looked hot.

"Bonjour Francoise," called Josephine's mother.

"Going to be a very hot day," Francoise sighed.

"It's going to be that, all right," Josephine's mother said as they walked, single file, down the dusty path. As they talked, Josephine fell behind. She let her feet move slowly in the warm, soft dust of the path and thought about those pennies she might get at the end of the day.

It was good to buy jelly rolls or candy but it would be a lot better to buy a doll—a real doll. Josephine never had a real doll. She'd had flower dolls—like those she played with that morning. But they were just hibiscus flower dolls.

Her mother had showed her how to make them when she was very small. She showed her how to take a tiny sliver of wood and stick it into a hibiscus bud. That was the head. The rest of the stick went into a big flower turned upside down. That made the skirt.

They were pretty, yes, and delicate too. But they wilted so soon. Josephine would make them fresh and bright in the morning, but by noon their heads would shrivel and their skirts would look torn and shaggy.

Josephine wished she could have a real doll someday.

After a while another woman turned into the dusty path with a load of baskets. "Bonjour Lucille," she called to Josephine's mother.

"Bonjour Gabrielle," came the answer.

"Going to be sizzling hot today!" Gabrielle said.

"Sure is," Josephine's mother agreed.

Josephine and her mother walked along the dusty path. Francoise and Gabrielle walked along not far behind. In a little while they met another woman with a big load of mangoes on her head.

"Bonjour Marie," said Josephine's mother.

"Fine morning to you," Marie said as she joined the group of women going to town. In a little while they met a man with a wheelbarrow full of grain. Soon they met other men too—men with burros or goats. One man tugged at a stubborn pig. Everybody had something to sell at the market. Nobody went with empty hands—except Josephine. When you go to market you've got to have something to sell.

Josephine was getting tired. She wanted to lie down in the shade of some palm trees along the edge of the path. She wanted a sip of cool water. She was almost sorry she'd agreed to go to the market. If she hadn't she would now be at home playing with her flower dolls. But even if she stayed at home there would be chores to do. She could just hear her mother saying—as she so often did —"Now Josephine, work is one thing and play is another. We got to get these brooms to market and we got to sell every one of them!"

Josephine wriggled her toes in the dusty path and hoped they would be there soon.

Around the bend in the road Josephine could smell the market place. It was a strong good smell of sweet fruit and vegetables, candies and frying pork, of goats and pigs and straw and dust.

Josephine walked faster now. She followed her mother to their favorite spot in a little patch of shade under a torn awning. Carefully Josephine's mother lowered the basket of little brooms from her head and set it before her as she sat down. Now her little shop was in order. She didn't have one thing more to do except sit and sell brooms until the sun went down.

"Now you run off, child," Josephine's mother said as she gave her a playful little push. "I have business to attend to."

Josephine wandered through the big, noisy market. All along the sides of the square were little shops where people were busy buying or selling or cooking or making things.

Josephine loved the shop with a sign that said, "The Fine Sweet Shop." It smelled of fresh baked goods—bread and cakes and little sweet tarts. Josephine watched the baker working in the little room just beyond. How busily and expertly he worked with the brightly-colored frostings—shaping, pushing, forming the delicious things to eat. How quickly he worked. What good use he made of everything around him! Nothing was wasted—nothing at all.

Next door was the butcher shop. The butcher was working hard too. All of his knives were gleaming and sharp. They flashed in the bright sunlight as he carefully carved his meats.

That was the way it was with all of the people who came to market. Everybody worked hard—nothing was wasted, everything was used.

Josephine had just turned away from the butcher shop when she bumped into an old man she had never seen before. He had a big stick and a very big straw hat—much bigger than those anyone else wore. On it were different little animals made of straw. There were monkeys and pigs, donkeys and roosters. Some of them had tiny, jingly bells attached or were decorated with bright strips of cloth.

Josephine almost lost her balance but then she felt two big strong hands holding her up. "Looks like you have bumped into good luck, young lady!" The old man cackled and pulled one of the little straw pigs off his hat. "Here, child," he said, "I don't want to see those big, frightened eyes of yours first thing this market day. I want to start off with a *smile*. Come on now, child. Let me see a good big smile. That's the *only* way to start off market day!"

Josephine smiled and said, "Thank you," as she took the pretty thing in her hand. She was about to run to her mother when she had a thought. She turned to the old man saying, "How did you learn to make little animals of straw like that?"

The old man cackled again and grinned broadly. He slapped his knee, straightened up and had a good long laugh.

"Why, child," he said, good-naturedly, "Nobody taught me how to do it. Nobody learned me how to do much of anything. I just used my 'magination!"

Toward afternoon the shadows started to get big. The cool, soft breeze started to drift in from the sea. Josephine ran back to where her mother was sitting in the shade of the torn awning.

"Look, maman, *look* what a man gave me!"

Josephine's mother took the pig and examined it closely. "Cute little thing," she said, but then she sighed wearily. Josephine saw that only about half of the brooms were gone. "Guess we better start getting home," her mother said as she felt around for her hat. "This just isn't much of a broom day!" But then she fished under her skirt for the little black bag where she kept her money. She pulled out a penny—just one penny. "I guess you need something sweet in your mouth before we start for home. Now—run off to that Fine Sweet Shop."

Josephine rushed to the candy and cake store. On her way she passed the stall where the dolls were sold. But she tried not to look at them, tried not to think about them. For one penny she could only get one piece of candy so she chose carefully. Finally she decided on a nice piece of hard, lime candy—tangy but sweet—and cool like the breeze that was softly blowing in from the sea.

The sun was setting. The wind from the sea grew stronger. Josephine thought that this was one of the best times of market day—just going home. In the east, the moon hung in the sky like a big, pale slice of melon. The palmettos whispered and scratched against each other in the evening sea breeze. And the dust of the road felt cool and soft and easy to walk on.

As soon as Josephine got home she ran to see her flower dolls. They were so wilted and ugly that she was sorry she had kept them. She swept them angrily off the table onto the floor and went to help her mother prepare dinner.

They ate baked yams, breadfruit, mangoes and had sugar cane for dessert. Josephine was so hungry that every bite tasted delicious. "Never saw a child eat so much in my life!" her mother said.

But after she had eaten, the only thing that she could think about was her bed. Lying down in a darkened corner of the room, she thought about the day just passed.

She thought about the long, dusty walk into town and the walk back under the moon that seemed even longer. She thought about all the people and the shops and the happy old man with the straw toys attached to his big hat. How clearly she could hear him saying in a laughing voice, "I just used my 'magination!"

Josephine reached out to feel in the pocket of her dress for the small straw pig. In the firelight she could only see its outlines but she could feel the smoothly-woven straw and try to imagine what it looked like.

Did Josephine have a " 'magination?" Maybe she did and maybe she didn't. She wondered how you got a 'magination if you didn't already have one. Josephine decided she had to find out if she had one. Just before she went to sleep she promised herself that she wouldn't let another day pass without finding out if she too had a 'magination.

The morning was still cool when Josephine awoke. She looked at the bright, long stripes of morning sunlight falling on the floor of their tiny one-room house. In the far corner of the room her mother was sleeping soundly on her bed of straw matting. Outside, the birds were busy calling to each other and getting their breakfasts. Far down near the shore she heard a man's voice shouting. He was probably a fisherman busy getting his boat ready to take out to sea.

Busy, busy, busy—people were getting busy. That made her remember. She too should be getting busy. She had to find out about her 'magination.

Josephine looked around the room again and again. She tried to make some 'magination thoughts come into her head. She tried very hard to think. To see if she could find something—or *two* different things—that she could make something *new* out of.

There in a corner were short, broken broom handles. Nearby were the scratchy straw parts of the brooms. And scissors and raffia. Josephine looked at them for a long time.

Almost before she knew what she was doing, Josephine jumped out of bed and tied one of the straw brooms to the broken brooms. Then she took a scissors and cut the straws short.

How funny it looked now—not like a broom at all but like a skirt.

"What are you doing there?" Her mother raised herself from her straw mat.

"Just playing."

"Just playing? Well, why are you playing with my good brooms? You answer me that!"

"But Maman, this one was broken. You never use the broken ones."

"But I use the rest of what you're using. Now you get dressed and get us some eggs. We got to have our breakfast!"

Josephine slid the little broom under her bed of mats and did as her mother told her. After that there was other work to do. She had to weed the vegetable garden and feed the chickens. During the heat of the day she slept for a long time. When she awoke in the late afternoon she thought maybe she would make some fresh flower dolls. But she didn't. She was tired of those old floppy, withery dolls. Toward evening it was time to go down to the shore to buy a piece of fish for their supper.

It was a day just like a lot of other days. But Josephine felt a new kind of happy feeling all through the day. She didn't understand why or how—but she felt it.

That night when Josephine went to bed she put the strange little broom next to her on the pillow. In the moonlight it looked very strange. It wasn't a doll—but it was *almost* a doll.

Josephine listened to the rising of the night sea wind. Sometimes it rattled their shaky little house so much that she thought it would fall down on her. She reached out and felt the strange little doll. She was glad it was there.

The sky was just starting to get light when Josephine heard the first rooster crowing. "Cocka-doodle-doo. Cocka-doodle-doo . . ." He was better than any clock because he woke her at just about the same time every morning. It was going to be a beautiful morning. But Josephine didn't have time to watch the long, bright fingers of sunlight crawl into the room today.

Without even thinking what she was doing, she ran to the shed where her mother kept some paint. She took an old brush and quickly covered the broom handle with black paint. She worked quickly without thinking very much how. She knew what she had to do. Something was telling her. She knew it was her 'magination giving out the orders.

As soon the the paint had dried, Josephine took some brightly-colored scraps of cloth that were left over from a dress Josephine's mother had made for her. One of the strips got tied around the middle of the broom-doll. The other was bound around her head in the same way that some of the women on the island bound their heads.

Josephine put the broom-doll down and looked at it. It was amazing what 'magination could tell you to do—no doubt about it! But something important was still missing. Josephine picked a long, feathery weed which made a fine-pointed brush. A good dab of red made the mouth. White showed where the eyes were.

Oh yes, now she was wonderful. She was a doll, a *real* doll. But she was more than a doll too. Just take her in your fingers and brush her back and forth and she worked hard cleaning and sweeping for you! What a good, busy kind of doll—not just one that lay around the house all day waiting to be taken care of.

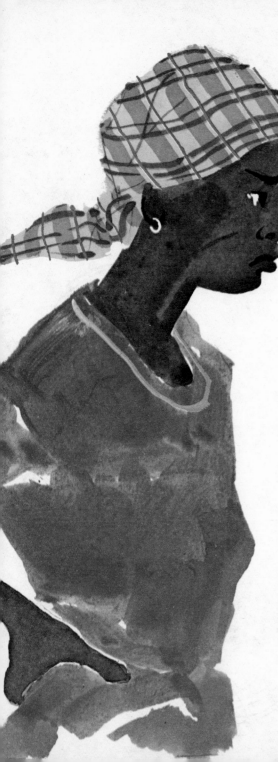

"Show me what you got there!" her mother's voice suddenly commanded from her dark corner of the room.

"I made a doll, Maman," Josephine said, taking the broom-doll to show her mother.

"Well . . . I never seen such a thing before." Her mother smiled. "Why, Josephine, you made yourself a mighty cute little doll."

"And Maman," Josephine said, "she's a good worker too!" She showed her mother what a good sweeping her doll could do.

"Yes—and a good worker too!" her mother agreed. "Josephine —you're a mighty smart little girl."

That afternoon they decided to make more broom-dolls so they could take them to market on Friday morning. Josephine's mother made the brooms as usual but Josephine painted their faces. And part of her job was also to tie on the brightly-colored pieces around their middles and on their heads.

When Friday morning came, Josephine and her mother were out of bed early and on their way into town while the morning was still cool. Hardly anyone was as the market place when they arrived. And it seemed that hours and hours went by—a long, long time— until anyone even came to see the strange little broom-dolls.

But then people began to come to look at them. And after they touched and admired the dolls they began to buy them. The children came too and begged their parents to buy some dolls. To them it didn't matter that the dolls were such good workers. They just liked the way they looked.

Josephine watched with delight as the little black purse began to fill with coins. She knew there would be candy this afternoon— perhaps more than ever before. She was just thinking about what she would choose when she saw a big shadow on the ground before her.

It was the shadow of the big straw hat that the old toy man wore. First he looked at the brooms, then at Josephine. He said, "I seen you before. You're the little girl who bumped into me the other day."

"Yes, I'm the girl," Josephine said.

The toy man's smile broadened. "And you made these dolls? I never seen such dolls before!"

"My mother and I made them," Josephine said.

He took one, turned it around admiringly. "Child—I'd say you got a powerful 'magination."

Josephine smiled.